THE
ACA

The Cursed
BALLET

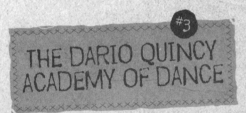

THE DARIO QUINCY ACADEMY OF DANCE

#3

The Cursed BALLET

BY MEGAN ATWOOD

MINNEAPOLIS

Darby Creek
A division of Lerner Publishing Group, Inc.
241 First Avenue North
Minneapolis, MN 55401 U.S.A.

Website address: www.lernerbooks.com

Cover and interior photographs © iStockphoto.com/Özgür Donmaz (main); © iStockphoto.com/Selahattin BAYRAM (paper background).

Main body text set in Janson Text LT Std 12/17.5.
Typeface provided by Linotype AG.

Library of Congress Cataloging-in-Publication Data

Atwood, Megan.
    The cursed ballet / by Megan Atwood.
        pages   cm. — (The Dario Quincy Academy of Dance ; #3)
    ISBN 978-1-4677-0932-3 (lib. bdg. : alk. paper)
    ISBN 978-1-4677-1629-1 (eBook)
    [1. Ballet dancing—Fiction. 2. Dance—Fiction. 3. Haunted places—Fiction. 4. Supernatural—Fiction.] I. Title.
    PZ7.A8952Cu 2013
    [Fic]—dc23   2012049710

Manufactured in the United States of America
1 – BP – 7/15/13

To my parents, for their constant support. And to Patrick, who literally held me up when I fell down. My love and gratitude to you.

Prologue

"Betsy, the answer is no. No, I say."

John Johnson III straightened out his perfectly fitted suit and brushed off imaginary lint. "My word is final."

He stared out the window, past Madame Puant's head. Someone who didn't know him well would have thought he was being cold. A person who looked more closely would see the sheen of sweat over his upper lip, the nervous tic in his eye.

And no wonder.

"Excuse. Me. Sir," Madame Puant said. Johnson flinched with each syllable. "If I remember correctly," Madame continued, "I am the ballet mistress at this school. And as such, I will decide which ballet we put on, thank you very much."

Her nose flared, the sharp intake of breath like the sound of a bull snorting. Johnson turned, sitting forward in his chair.

"Betsy, be reasonable. This ballet hasn't been performed in—"

"Thirty years. Yes, I know, John. Which is exactly why it's time to do it again."

Madame Puant began shuffling papers on her desk. A clear dismissal.

"As the owner of this school and this building, I have to insist you not go forward with this production. Now, I don't believe, ahem . . . I don't hold to the idea that this place is cursed, but neither you nor I can deny that when the company at this school performs *Giselle*, someone gets hurt. Do you want that on your head, Betsy?"

Madame Puant stood up slowly and imperiously. "You brought me here for a reason, John. I do not subscribe to curses, or to the supernatural, and I know in my heart of hearts that it's time we put such nonsense to bed. We will do *Giselle*. And with the ballet gods as my witness, not one of my girls is going to get hurt."

The fire in her eyes burned through Johnson's silk vest and scorched his stomach. He stood up to leave but turned around before he reached the door, the tailored suit moving around him like a second skin.

"Betsy, I hope to God you're right."

Madame Puant sat back down in her chair and watched through the window as John Johnson III stepped into his Bentley and drove off.

A person who didn't know her well would think she was calm and composed. But a person who looked more closely would see Madame Puant's fire begin to slowly flicker out.

Chapter 1

"Get off my ribbon."

Ophelia shoved Kayley, and Kayley tumbled into Madeleine, who bumped into Sophie and Emma. All five girls began to giggle.

Kayley rolled her eyes. "Good lord, Ophelia. This is ballet class, not rugby practice!"

Kayley sat down, tucking one leg under her and keeping one knee pointed up in one fluid motion, then finished tying her pointe shoe. When she was finished, she put her foot over

Ophelia's ribbon again.

Ophelia stared at her with daggers in her eyes, and Kayley burst out laughing. Ophelia reluctantly smiled.

Sophie, who was doing a splits stretch, said, "What's going on with you, Ophelia? Long night? Did you go out with a boooyyyy?" She shared a smile with Emma.

Among all the girls, Ophelia was definitely the most daring. She managed to meet boys from in town more often than the others, and she would often sneak out for dates. They never lasted long, though. Ophelia breathed, ate, and slept dance. No townie boy ever understood that.

Ophelia breathed out in exasperation, "No. It's not all about boys, you know!"

Madeleine grinned slowly. "Just most of the time, right?"

The rest of the girls cracked up. Ophelia ignored them. She was nervous, but she didn't want them to know. She could feel Kayley looking at her.

"No, it's *not* a boy. Ophelia knows

something," Kayley said. "OK, Ophelia, spill."

Ophelia had been dying all morning to share her information. She'd tried hard to keep it in—having a secret was delicious—but she couldn't anymore, especially since Kayley was like a clairvoyant witch and knew it anytime Ophelia was hiding something.

"All right," Ophelia said. "Here's what happened. The other day, I heard Madame talking to that owner guy. And I swear—now, I could be wrong—but I swear I heard them talking about *Giselle*! I think Dario Quincy might be putting on *Giselle*!"

Madeleine looked thrilled and clapped her hands, but Sophie, Emma, and Kayley were silent.

Ophelia exhaled in frustration. "Oh, come on, you guys. You don't really believe in those rumors, do you? Like a bunch of idiots?"

Kayley looked at Sophie and Emma. "What about the little ghost hunt you took us on a couple months ago? You know, for the ghost who was stealing our trinkets?"

Ophelia waved her hand. Kayley could

be such a stickler for facts sometimes. "Oh, that was ages ago. And anyway, I didn't really believe it was a ghost. It was just something to do! Something less boring than sitting around in the dorms."

She reached in her bag for a hairpin, then wrapped the hair around her bun and stuck the pin in, scraping her head.

"Madeleine held her hands out and shrugged. "OK, I'm lost. What's going on?"

Ophelia rolled her eyes again. "Oh, these yahoos think that performances of *Giselle* are cursed here at the academy. It's been a rumor since before I came here. The school hasn't put it on in years." She stood up and threw her leg on the barre. Class would start any minute, and she wasn't feeling the least bit limber.

Kayley stood up too, then Sophie, Emma, and Madeleine.

"Thirty years to be exact, Ophelia," Kayley said. "And I suppose you think you'll get the role of Giselle?"

Ophelia raised an eyebrow and worked to suppress a smile. Of course, she thought she'd get the role. She was the best dancer in the company, with maybe the exception of Madeleine. But she just had a feeling in her stomach that she would be Giselle. She'd wanted to play that part since she was ten, the first time she'd seen it done.

Kayley went on: "Yeah, well, the last three times this company has put on *Giselle*—the only three times—the ballerina who played her died. *Died*, Ophelia. Do you want to die?"

Ophelia twirled around and stared at her. "Of course, I don't. But I *won't*. It's just a stupid rumor."

Emma shook her head. "I don't know Ophelia. I mean, why now? Why are we putting it on now?"

Just then, Madame Puant walked into the room with the piano player, Patrick. She knocked her cane on the ground three times, signifying the start of dance class. "Barre exercises, everyone!"

Ophelia took a quick peek at Kayley and Madeleine, who were sharing a look. It didn't matter. If they were going to do *Giselle*, Ophelia wanted the lead more than anything else. It didn't matter what the other girls thought. She held onto the barre and followed Madame's warm-up instructions: tendu, back-side-front, plié, then relevé.

As they warmed up, Madame took a breath and then said, "All right, class. We have decided on our next ballet."

Ophelia could feel the whole class breathe in with anticipation. This was one of the best parts of being at the school—learning, rehearsing, and putting on a ballet. What every dancer at the school came for.

"We are going to perform *Giselle*."

The class erupted in talk and chatter. Speaking over everyone, Madame yelled, "And our Giselle will be none other than Ophelia."

Ophelia broke out in a huge grin. But the class had gone silent. Silent as a morgue.

As if they were grieving for her already.

Chapter 2

After class, Ophelia could hardly stop smiling. Kayley, Sophie, Emma, and Madeleine kept throwing worried glances her way, but she ignored them.

Giselle. Her dream.

As she walked out the door, Madame tapped her arm and whispered, "My office. After class tonight."

Ophelia nodded and noticed a bead of sweat on Madame's temple. Well. It was hot in the studio.

Through breakfast and all her classes, Ophelia could feel the stares on her. Not that she minded. She'd never admit it to anyone, but she loved the attention. Still, she started to feel uneasy.

In French that day, Mr. Beauchamp gave her looks of pity and let her get away with speaking English.

In history, Ms. Traysor gave her back a paper: She saw a *B* scratched out and an *A* written to the side.

At lunch she dropped a fork, and the girl next to her ran away crying, "It's already started!"

Now Ophelia was irritated. The curse was a stupid rumor started by jealous girls who hadn't been given the part of Giselle. But Ophelia was used to the jealousy. So for the rest of the day and through afternoon ballet class, she kept her chin up high, ignoring the little feeling that made her squirm ever so slightly. It was just a rumor.

Still, she was glad to go talk to Madame. No matter how intimidating Madame Puant was, she always made Ophelia feel better, just by her presence.

Ophelia entered Madame's office, dropped her bag on the floor, and sat in one of the gigantic leather chairs. Madame hadn't arrived yet, but Ophelia had been at the academy for three years now, so she felt comfortable splaying out and waiting. As she wiggled one foot, impatient to get the meeting going, she scanned the top of Madame's desk.

The normally tidy stretch of oak was littered with papers. Ophelia stood up to take a look, checking behind her to make sure Madame wasn't coming. Many of the papers were stamped with an official-looking stationery; what looked like old newspaper clippings peppered the rest of the desk. She leaned in closer to get a better look.

Curious, Ophelia leaned even closer and saw the corner of a book sticking out from underneath the papers. The pages of the book were old and yellow; some sort of ribbon stuck out from between two of them. A journal.

"Please have a seat, Ms. DuBois."

Ophelia jumped from hearing Madame's voice. The ballet mistress walked briskly past Ophelia and began cleaning up the desk. Ophelia stumbled back into the leather chair and stammered, "Hi-hey, Mada—"

Ophelia's voice trailed off as she realized how ridiculous she sounded. She cleared her throat and waited for Madame to finish cleaning off the desk.

Madame opened one of the ornately carved drawers and placed the papers inside, setting the journal on top. Then she produced a key from a necklace around her neck and locked the drawer.

She sat down and looked Ophelia in the eye, startling her.

Why did Ophelia feel like she was in trouble?

"You asked to talk to me, Madame?"

Madame continued to stare at her, crossing her hands and tapping her index fingers.

Ophelia squirmed a little in her seat.

Tap.

Tap.

Tap.

Now Ophelia was getting nervous. She wondered if maybe she'd been spotted during some night out with some stupid townie boy. How could that have happened?

Madame sat back suddenly and rested her arms on the chair, looking for all the world like a queen in a throne. "I won't beat around the bush, Ophelia. You've heard the rumors about *Giselle*, I take it?"

Ophelia relaxed her shoulders and felt relief flow down her spine. She nodded.

"Well, I don't take to such fancy." Madame waved her hand dismissively, and Ophelia nodded again.

Madame's brown eyes found Ophelia's once more, and this time, they were burning. "But, my dear Ms. DuBois, many others do take to such fancy. And unfortunately, incidences have, uh . . . fueled . . . this nonsense.

"What I *do* believe is that our beliefs have a way of manifesting themselves. Of causing the very thing we wish to avoid. Do you understand what I'm saying?"

Ophelia furrowed her eyebrows. "I . . . don't

think so, Madame."

Madame stood up. "What I'm saying, Ophelia, is that curse or not, for whatever reason, this ballet presents a danger to our school. A danger for you in particular."

Ophelia felt herself shrink away from the intensity of Madame's gaze.

Madame continued: "So, I need to know: Are you afraid? Would you like me to rescind the part of Giselle? Tell me now, and we will not put on this ballet."

It was Ophelia's turn to stand up. "Madame," she said, crossing her arms, "I don't think you've ever found me afraid of anything. And I *will* be dancing Giselle. Better than anyone else here has before."

She stuck out her chin. No way would she let some stupid rumor ruin the greatest role of her life so far.

Madame chuckled and walked to the other side of the desk.

"No, Ophelia, you are not afraid. That bravery and your dancing are the two reasons I believe we can do this ballet. You are exactly the Giselle we need. I do believe you are strong enough. But mark my words: if there's even a *hint* of something untoward, the show is off."

She patted Ophelia's shoulder and said, "Now, go get supper. You must be starved after our practice, and you must take proper care of yourself. I want my Giselle in good health."

With that, Madame scooted Ophelia out the door, leaving Ophelia a little more baffled but mostly thrilled to known Madame believed in her.

Chapter 3

That night Ophelia couldn't sleep. She was way too wired. She'd been too late for dinner after her talk with Madame Puant, and anyway, she didn't feel like answering questions from her friends, so she stayed in and watched clips from different productions of *Giselle*.

She loved the costuming, the dance steps, the story... a prince parading around as a peasant for a laugh, the peasant girl who falls in love with him and dies from a broken heart.

Ophelia decided the girl was pretty dumb for falling for something like that, but she loved Giselle's death scene and all the footwork involved. She was going to kick butt at this ballet.

Around midnight, Ophelia couldn't stand it anymore. She'd watched enough ballet for the night—time to do some.

She pulled on her leotard and tights, wrapped a gauzy skirt around her waist, and slipped on some Uggs to warm her legs. Grabbing her bag, she opened the door and looked both ways down the dark hall.

No one around. The candle-shaped lights in the hallway flickered off and on, throwing shadows on the floor.

She tiptoed out, even though she was standing on carpet, and then, light as air, ran to the studio, up the stairs, and through the huge doorway that always stood open.

This wasn't the first time Ophelia had snuck into the studio to practice. But even so, the place looked dark and menacing, window-shaped blocks of moonlight the only thing lighting the floor. Ophelia caught a glimpse of someone and jumped and squealed, putting her hands over her mouth.

It was just her. In the mirror. Still, with her heart beating so fast she could hardly stand it, she wondered if late-night practice was a good idea.

She shrugged it off. She was already there at the studio, so she might as well use it.

She did some big stretches, loving the way her body felt as it started limbering up. Once she finished, she did some barre work, deep pliés, relevés, tendus, the usual warm-up. Then some in-place jumps to pliés, and she was ready to put on her pointe shoes.

After a few spins and some relevés en pointe, Ophelia felt completely warmed up.

She thought about *Giselle*'s opening scene. Just from watching clips, she knew the first sequence. The steps were pretty easy, but they included a lot of jumping and bouncing. The scene showed Giselle's love for dancing. Ophelia could relate.

She pretended to come out of her cottage

door, and then the dance took her over. She *was* Giselle.

Round the classroom, dance to audience, kicks, jetés, pure love . . . Ophelia felt all of it. Though the steps weren't in the dance, she added five fouettés, spotting herself in the darkened mirror, her breath coming fast, and feeling the dance through her whole being. Her head whipped around, finding the same place in the mirror for every turn:

Spot.

Spot.

Spot.

Spot.

Spot.

On her last spot, Ophelia fell over and landed on the floor on her hands and knees.

Someone else was in the studio.

She clambered up to see a dark form between the squares of illuminated floor. A soft, male voice said, "Don't be afraid. I didn't mean to startle you."

The voice didn't belong to any of the boy dancers that Ophelia knew at the school.

Ophelia felt naked in front of this stranger. She backed up against the mirror.

"Who the hell are you? And why are you in this studio?"

The boy came into the light.

He wore some seriously weird clothes, as if he were in the early 1900s: short pants to his knees—Ophelia was pretty sure they were called knickerbockers—and a tuniclike shirt with buttons all the way down one side.

He also wore a cap that Ophelia knew was from the olden times; squat to the head with a bill that stuck out a bit. She wondered if she was dreaming.

He put his hand out. "Forgive me. But your dancing was so beautiful."

The boy was good looking, Ophelia had to admit. Like, really good looking. He had dark hair under his hat, thick eyebrows, and long lashes. And he had a strong jawline and startling eyes of a color that Ophelia couldn't make out in the light. He looked to be about seventeen or eighteen, right around Ophelia's age.

She stuck a hip out and put her hand on it, but her voice softened a little. "Yeah, yeah, thanks. What are you doing here? Who are you?"

And then, because she couldn't help herself, she said, "And *what* are you wearing?"

The boy chuckled, then took a step forward into the darkness between the lighted squares on the floor.

"I'm Devon," he said, with some sort of accent Ophelia couldn't place. Then he took another step forward, into the light. "This is my school. And these are the clothes I wear to dance. May I dance with you?"

After another step, Ophelia could see his eyes. They were pale gray with dark rings around the pupils. She couldn't stop looking at them.

When he smiled, she couldn't help but smile back. He put his hand out to her.

Tentatively, she reached her hand out in return. His palm was strangely cold, but he pulled her close to him and Ophelia's whole body tingled.

The boy smelled vaguely dusty, like he'd just walked through an old library, but there was also a deep, woodsy, spicy smell lingering. It made Ophelia just a little dizzy.

In her ear, he whispered, "You are Giselle, no?"

She didn't trust herself to speak, so she nodded.

"Well, I am your prince, come to dance with you."

With that, he led her around the room in a pas de deux, big dancing movements that covered the entire dance floor.

Ophelia couldn't catch her breath. His dancing was beautiful and fluid, like nothing she'd ever experienced. And the woodsy smell kept her leaning in close.

After what seemed like only seconds but must have been a quarter of an hour, Devon pulled away and stepped back. Ophelia stood there, struck dumb, her chest heaving and her body still tingling.

He began to walk toward the door, and Ophelia almost called out to him. But he turned around and said, "Tomorrow night? Same time?"

All Ophelia could do was nod. And then the boy of her dreams walked out of the room.

Chapter 4

Ophelia got back to her room at two o'clock and couldn't get back to sleep. She could smell Devon on her leotard and on her hair. Every time she moved her head, she could almost feel him near her. Never before had she felt this way. Ever.

In ballet class that morning, though she hadn't gotten any sleep, she danced the Giselle part so well that even Madame was surprised. She hardly needed any help on the choreography and felt light as air. Even her smile, which Madame had called wooden in past performances, was genuine and huge, and it stayed on her face well after she finished dancing.

At the end of class, Kayley, Madeleine, Sophie, and Emma came up to her.

"All right, what gives?" Kayley said.

Ophelia shrugged, but the smile came back.

"I don't know what you're talking about," she said, almost giggling.

Kayley exchanged looks with Sophie and Emma while Madeleine said, with a sly smile, "All right, who is he?"

How did she know? Ophelia wondered. For reasons she couldn't put into words, she wanted to keep Devon all to herself. She didn't want anyone else seeing him or dancing with him. The very thought made her whole body tense up. She turned on Madeleine, grabbing her arm. "Who do you mean, he? What were you doing last night?"

Madeleine stepped backward with each of Ophelia's words. Ophelia was immediately sorry—what was she doing? Madeleine had just asked a simple, innocent question. She was always nice that way.

Ophelia let go of Madeleine's arm, and Madeleine began rubbing it right away.

"I'm so sorry," Ophelia said. "I just . . ."

The others stared at her, their faces shocked and angry. Kayley especially looked upset.

"It just was a long night, that's all," Ophelia mumbled. Then she grabbed her bag and ran out of the room.

Somehow, for the rest of the day, she would have to avoid her friends, Ophelia thought. Before they had her committed.

Chapter 5

Ophelia faked sick for the rest of the afternoon. She even skipped her second ballet class, which she never did. She just couldn't face Madeleine and the rest of the girls.

But there was something else: she didn't want to tell them about Devon, and she didn't think she could keep it a secret around her friends.

All day, Devon had been all Ophelia could think of. The way he guided her around the dance floor, his smooth steps, and his spicy smell . . . those gorgeous eyes.

A little thrill skipped down her back. Tonight.

By eleven thirty, Ophelia was pacing in her room. She'd tried to take in more of *Giselle* but couldn't concentrate. She wanted to dance, not sit back and watch.

Finally, she couldn't take it anymore. Ophelia snuck up to the studio and began the warm-ups. Soon she was lost in her work, and when she turned around from a particularly high jeté, she saw him there. In the shadows.

He stepped forward and smiled at her. He wore the same clothes as he did the night before, and even from across the room, Ophelia could once again smell the dusty, woodsy, spicy smell that meant Devon. The moonlight shined across his eyes, it seemed, making them glow with an otherworldly light.

Ophelia smiled back, and nerves sparked like fireworks through her whole body.

"My Giselle," he said and held out his hand to her.

She took his hand, and they danced again.

Ophelia had never felt so at home, so in tune, with another person. Through dips and holds, turns and leaps, they held onto each other, dancing like they were one, completely in synch.

It was intoxicating.

As before, Devon stopped dancing after what seemed like seconds but had to have been much longer and looked into Ophelia's eyes. But this time, he stepped closer instead of stepping away.

Ophelia's heart began to race. He was so good looking that she thought her knees would go weak. Devon ran his hand down her cheek.

"Giselle," he murmured. "You are mine, always."

In one swoop, he pulled her even closer and kissed her on the mouth.

The fireworks inside Ophelia exploded.

He stepped back and said, "Tomorrow night, then. Same time?" He smiled at her gently.

All Ophelia could do was nod.

Chapter 6

For the next four days, the same thing happened:

Ophelia went to classes, ballet, and school; ignored her friends; and danced with Devon.

Mealtimes were the hardest, so she just started skipping them altogether, grabbing a granola bar here and there from snack machines, snagging the occasional muffin before the meal crowd came in.

Not that it mattered. Ophelia wasn't even close to hungry.

All she could think about was Devon and their dances. They hadn't even had one real conversation, but Ophelia didn't mind. The dancing was enough for her.

Each day in ballet class, she danced as if she were alone with Devon, and her dancing had never been better. She even heard Madame describe it as "exquisite" over the phone when she passed by Madame's office.

Even though the long nights were taking their toll, she felt energized like never before. She knew she had big bags under her eyes, that she'd lost weight, but she didn't care.

The only thing that mattered was Devon and the way he made her feel.

After the last ballet class of the day on Friday and after Ophelia had sprinted out of the studio to avoid her friends and wait alone in her room for her time with Devon, she heard a knock on her door.

For a ridiculous second, she thought it might be him. She ran to the door and flung it open.

It was Kayley. And Kayley didn't look

happy. Her arms crossed, she said, "Can I come in?"

Ophelia didn't even try to hide her disappointment. But now that Kayley was there, Ophelia didn't know how she'd get rid of her, so she opened the door wider and gestured for Kayley to come in.

Her frown remained as Kayley strode over to the dressing table chair and sat down. Ophelia remained standing, crossing her arms and tapping her feet, her eyebrows up.

For a moment, the two of them just stared at each other.

"Well?" Ophelia said.

Kayley sighed and knit her hands together, looking down with an expression so forlorn, Ophelia actually felt bad for a second.

"What's going on with you, Ophelia?" Kayley finally asked.

"I don't know what you're talking about." She turned around and pretended to shuffle things on her desk, though she hadn't done her homework all week. A note from one of her teachers atop the pile of papers gave Ophelia two days to finish an assignment or she'd get a zero. But all of that seemed so trivial—what did any of it matter when there was dancing to be done?

Kayley shook her head and fiddled with a brush on the dressing table. When she finally looked up, there were tears in her eyes.

"You've been disappearing every day. You don't talk to any of us or eat with any of us. You look like crap. I know something is up. Just like you knew something was up when I took those shoes. This house has a way of . . . isolating you. You know that."

Ophelia waved her hand. "Oh, come on! That's ridiculous. And anyway, I'm fine. I just feel like being alone right now."

"I know you believe in this stuff," Kayley said. "Remember the ghost hunt?"

"I didn't actually believe a ghost was taking our stuff! I just wanted an adventure."

Kayley took two steps toward her, her eyes earnest and concerned. "Whatever adventure you're on right now, Ophelia, it is doing something strange to you. You look like your life force is draining or something. And you're not talking to your friends. That means something is up.

"Whatever you believe about the house, know this: Don't always believe what you see or hear. Question anything that seems a little strange. Because in this house, it probably is. And with the curse of *Giselle*...well, you especially have to watch your back. Until then, whether you want it or not, Madeleine, Sophie, Emma, and I are watching your back."

Before Ophelia could respond, Kayley marched out of the room.

Ophelia stared at the door in disbelief. Was that some sort of threat? Had her friends been spying on her? Did they know about Devon?

Panic gripped her as she searched her mind, trying to find a time when someone might have spotted her. But it couldn't be. Devon would have noticed, even if Ophelia hadn't.

How dare the girls decide they knew what was best for her! They were jealous of her dancing. They were jealous that she'd found something (someone) else to take up her time, that she no longer involved herself in their petty lives and the school's petty goings-on.

Jealous.

Rage raced through Ophelia. She needed some distraction before her midnight date with Devon. She tapped her mouth with her fingers, trying to think of what could work.

Riffling through her closet, she found the old box she kept full of yearbooks, show programs, and old notebooks. She dug through the box and came up with what she was looking for: a journal. Her mom had given her the journal when she came to Dario Quincy three years ago. But since Ophelia wasn't much for feelings, she'd tossed the journal aside with a snort and hadn't thought of it since.

Now, though, she felt this was the perfect time to put down her thoughts. She felt compelled to write about Devon. He was so ethereal that she was afraid he would disappear. She wanted to write down everything he said or did, everything he made her feel. And she wanted to write about her friends and how strange they were acting.

She opened up the diary and wrote the first words that came to mind:

My friends are acting strange, and I know it is because they are jealous. The only thing that gives me comfort right now is Devon. Dancing with him makes the whole world disappear. I find that I long for him every single night—I wait with bated breath to be reunited with him. He feeds my soul like nothing else can. I needn't eat nor sleep, for Devon is my nourishment. Those around me only serve as distractions, and they will never understand this need I have for him, this yearning that consumes me.

After an hour and a cramped hand—who ever writes longhand anymore instead of using a computer?—she read over the first few lines. Crinkling her forehead, she reread them. The words were exactly how she felt, only somehow, they didn't sound like her.

A trickle of nervousness ran through her. Kayley's words about the strangeness of the house echoed around Ophelia's head. Then she happened to glance at the clock. Eleven fifty.

She jumped up and got ready to sprint to the dance studio.

Devon would be there, and she couldn't be late.

Chapter 7

In ballet class that Monday, Ophelia was on cloud nine again. She and Devon danced the entire weekend, ending with a kiss that made Ophelia shiver every time she thought about it. Part of her wondered if that was because of his always-cold hands, but she knew it was because of something else: she was falling in love.

Ophelia stayed far away from Kayley, Madeleine, Sophie, and Emma during practice, but she could still notice their quick glances and their worried expressions.

As Ophelia relaced her shoe, hanging back from the center of the room for the third time, Madeleine tiptoed toward her. When Ophelia stood up, she was face-to-face with Madeleine's worried, kind eyes. Darkness threatened to overtake Ophelia—she must have stood up too fast. But the darkness receded into little points of light, and she looked at Madeleine impatiently.

"What?" she whispered to Madeleine, in no mood to deal with whatever nonsense Madeleine was going to spout.

"We're worried about you," Madeleine whispered back.

Ophelia's eyes turned cold. "I don't need your worry." She flipped around to the barre and worked her leg high up behind her, kicking it out and staring at the mirror in front of her so she wouldn't have to look at Madeleine.

Mirror-Madeleine looked helplessly at the girls across the room. Ophelia felt bad for just a moment. Then Madeleine's turn to dance came, and she toed her way to the stage.

Ophelia decided just to note all the looks the girls gave her or gave one another about her for further diary entries. She could document their jealousy in the pages of the diary. Then she'd have a date with Devon that was untainted by her frustration with her friends. What kind of friends were they, anyway? To not give her space when she needed it? She would have to find a way to avoid them more often, if that were possible.

Ophelia was relieved to see that Madeleine didn't come back toward her once she'd run off the stage. The corps danced on. Ophelia continued to stretch at the barre, getting ready to dance Giselle's death scene. As she bent over her knee to keep limber, a wave of blackness swept in. Dizziness overtook her. She stood up slowly, feeling her heartbeat thumping hard.

She took deep breaths, willing the dizziness to go away. This was one of Ophelia's favorite scenes to dance—no way was she going to miss it.

Madame Puant waved the corps off the stage

and called to Patrick to play the death scene. She looked at Ophelia and said, "All right. Are you ready?"

Ophelia nodded, aware that all eyes were on her. Madame squinted at her, a look of concern passing over her face. Ophelia gathered herself up and took center stage, fighting back the darkness that still lingered in her peripheral vision.

Patrick started the music, and the feeling of the dance took Ophelia over. Everything she felt for Devon came through in her movements. She thought of the agony of losing him and tears almost started flowing. She used that pain, converting all the sadness, loneliness, and despair into a haunting performance. In that moment, Ophelia was Giselle.

As she came out of a particularly hard turn, she caught a glimpse of someone in the open studio door. A woman, stately and well dressed, stared at her with an intensity that could rival Madame. The woman wore a long, tailored coat and small diamond earrings. Her hair was tied back in a severe twist. Her dark eyes held on to Ophelia's until Ophelia forgot where she was and snapped her out of her reverie.

In that moment, the room went black. The last thing she heard was a voice say, "She's falling."

Chapter 8

When Ophelia woke up, she was in a bed of some sort with an IV hooked up to her. The stern, bright eyes of the academy nurse hovered over her.

"Well, hello, Sleeping Beauty," Nurse John said.

Ophelia struggled to sit up, but Nurse John pushed her back down gently. "Nuh-uh, I don't think so. You blacked out and had a nasty fall in class. You'll be in here for a while."

Ophelia groaned and moved her knee. She could feel a scrape rubbing against her tights. And then panic overtook her.

"What time is it?"

Nurse John furrowed his eyebrows and said, "Ten P.M. Why?"

Ophelia sighed and sank back. She hadn't missed Devon. She was cutting it too close for comfort, but at least she hadn't missed midnight.

"I'm just wondering how long I was out," she answered.

Nurse John frowned and then checked her IV and moved some things on the table beside her. A large can of coconut water stood on Ophelia's table. The nurse cracked it open.

"Well, you passed out around five thirty, then came to about six when they brought you in here. Then you fell asleep and have been sleeping ever since. You clearly needed it."

He brought a chair next to her bed and interlaced his fingers, his expression kind but worried.

"Ophelia, when was the last time you ate?"

Ophelia was startled. She hadn't even thought

of food. At the mention of it, her stomach growled like it had been called to life. She thought for a second. Had she eaten that day?

"I don't know."

Nurse John sighed and nodded. "Yes, that's what I thought." He cleared his throat and said, "Ophelia, dancing is a tough business. It's hard on your body, especially classical ballet. To do the work, you have to be properly fueled . . ."

Light dawned on Ophelia. This was Nurse John's eating-disorder spiel. The coconut water, the close talking . . . Nurse John thought Ophelia had stopped eating on purpose.

Ophelia had a hard time not snorting. She knew a lot of ballet dancers had eating disorders. It's not like that was news. The competition, the stress to keep a lean body, the perfectionism . . . Well, it was a perfect storm.

But that had never been Ophelia, luckily. She liked food a lot, but not too much, and she always ate when she needed to. Otherwise, well, she would pass out. And then she almost hit herself in the head; that's exactly what had happen.

Now she just had to convince Nurse John that it wasn't a disorder, just a mistake. Otherwise, she'd heard what happens to girls like that. They'd spend days trapped in the nurse's office while he watches them eat. And if things don't get better, they go off to treatment. Ophelia had seen it more than once.

She thought all of that was a great solution. Until now.

Nurse John's voice reached Ophelia's ears, ". . . overnight, at least for tonight."

"Wait, what?"

"You're going to stay overnight tonight, just so I can make sure your electrolytes are balanced and you're properly fueled."

"But I can't tonight! I have to dance Giselle!"

Nurse John patted her shoulder. "And you will. But we have to get you better. And we have to make sure you eat. So tomorrow, you can dance!"

Ophelia couldn't tell him the real reason— she'd miss dancing Giselle with Devon. Dancing at class was a faint second. But the determination in Nurse John's eyes told Ophelia that she'd be doing exactly as he said.

Tears coursed down her face.

"There, there," said Nurse John. "It's only a dance."

Ophelia sobbed. Not a dance. It was love.

Chapter 9

Despite her heartbreak at not seeing Devon, Ophelia was surprised at how hard she slept that night.

When she woke up the next morning, she ate a huge breakfast, making Nurse John smile.

And making herself feel much better, she realized. Ophelia hadn't realized how awful she felt. She had been too wrapped up in Devon.

The familiar panic shot through Ophelia, but the feeling was more muted than it had been the day before. Missing one night with Devon didn't seem as dire now. She had to remind herself to eat—she felt better than she had all week.

For the first time in days too, she wondered how Madeleine, Sophie, Kayley, and Emma were doing.

Nurse John gave her a pass to go to classes, but not to ballet practice. When Ophelia walked into civics, she smiled at Kayley and the girls. They all gave tentative smiles back. And when lunch came around, Ophelia sat at the table with them, heaping her plate with lasagna.

She dug in to her dish and said "Holy crap, this is good!" as the other girls stared at her.

"How are you feeling?" Madeleine asked. "That was so scary in class the other day when you fell."

Sophie nodded. "Yeah, you had a little seizure. Like you were possessed or something."

Ophelia swallowed. Nurse John hadn't said anything about that. No wonder he was concerned. She was slightly embarrassed but shook it off.

"I'm fine, now. I just hadn't eaten enough."

She took another bite of her lasagna.

"Why not, though?" Kayley said. "No offense, but you looked like death. Your eyes were dark, and you seemed tired all week. Are you going to tell us what's going on?"

Ophelia thought for a moment and then put down her fork. She wondered if she should tell them about Devon after all. She'd been dying to share her secret with them, but something always seemed to hold her back. Some part of her that wanted Devon all to herself. As she looked around at her friends' faces, though, she knew she shouldn't hold back.

She leaned in. "OK, there's something going on, but you have to promise not to tell. *And . . .*" she looked at Kayley, "don't be judgmental. Promise?"

Emma and Sophie nodded simultaneously, and Madeleine said yes. Kayley remained silent until Ophelia looked her way. Finally, Kayley nodded.

"Right. So, I've met a boy," Ophelia whispered. She sat back, that old twinge of excitement sparking through her.

"That's it?" Kayley said.

Ophelia nodded impatiently. How could she explain Devon? "Yeah, that's it. Only, he's more than a boy. He's . . . he's a dancer. And he makes me feel . . ."

Emma's eyes widened, and she said, "Ophelia, are you in love?"

A smile from out of nowhere burst from Ophelia. "Yes," she said, trying hard to keep her voice down. "Yes, I think I'm in love."

Kayley rolled her eyes. "Emma, you always think people are in love. Ophelia, how in love could you be with someone you met, what, like a week ago?"

"You wouldn't know anything about him," Ophelia said. "I know how I feel about Devon. He's . . . he's perfect."

"How did you meet him?" Madeleine asked.

Ophelia got excited again. "He just showed up one night while I was practicing. In the studio. And he can dance . . . he knows *Giselle*! When he kisses me—"

She cut herself off. It was not like her to

gush, not like her at all. She felt her face go red.

But Kayley's face was red too. "So. Let me get this straight. You're the star of a cursed ballet where the main character—you—always dies. And some strange boy shows up when you're dancing, and you don't think twice about it. Have you guys gone out on a date? Is he from town? Why is he just showing up here at the studio? If we've never seen him before, he's clearly not a student. How does he know *Giselle*? Where does he dance?"

Ophelia sat back, flustered and angry. She realized she didn't know how to answer any of those questions. "You're just jealous," she said, standing up. "You're always jealous of me. Jealous of how I can dance and jealous that I've met the man of my dreams."

Kayley stood up too, scraping her chair against the floor. Conversation across the lunchroom stopped. "You're being an idiot, Ophelia! This isn't like you at all! What do you know about this guy?"

Ophelia grabbed her bag and walked away furiously. After a few steps, she turned around and said, "I know that I'd rather be with him than hang out with any of you losers."

And she stomped away to her room.

Chapter 10

As much as Ophelia didn't want to admit it, Kayley's questions nagged at her.

Where did Devon come from? How did he just show up? And his clothes . . . why hadn't she asked him any questions? He just appeared, and they danced.

Ophelia took out her diary and wrote down everything that had happen, all the feelings she felt. When she looked at the clock, it was already eight. She'd missed dinner. It didn't matter. She wasn't hungry again. Thinking about Devon had ruined any appetite she might have had.

After putting the diary away, she thought about what to do. Kayley was right—the whole thing with Devon was a little weird. But she just couldn't believe anything was wrong with him. She just needed to ask him some questions, that's all. Maybe even ask him out—out of the studio and into public. She smiled at the thought. She'd love to show him off, although she didn't want any other girls to get any ideas. He was hers and hers alone.

She thought.

She chewed her fingernails. They *were* going out, right?

Bouncing her knee, she tried hard to distract herself until midnight.

Finally, at twenty to twelve, Ophelia ran up to the studio. She did halfhearted warm-ups and felt her heart beat hard again. She wished she'd eaten. She still felt weak from the day before, and as she did her stretches, she started feeling woozy. Just as darkness threatened at the corners of her eyes again, she saw him.

As usual, he stood in the moonlight. She walked to him, ignoring her advancing lightheadedness.

"My Giselle," he said and took her hand, pulling her to him. She melted into him, breathing in his woodsy, spicy smell. Wasn't there something she was supposed to do? She tried hard to think of it, but all she could do was feel his closeness, his hand on her back, the muscles along his arm, the cold breath on her cheek. His eyes bored into hers, and she couldn't think of anything else but the dancing.

Ophelia stumbled a little during one turn, and for a split second, Devon's face contorted in anger. It was enough to snap Ophelia out of whatever trance she was in.

She stepped back from him. "Where are you from?" she asked.

He looked confused. "I'm from here. Now come. We must dance that last part again. You ruined it." He waved his hand, urging her forward.

Ophelia wanted more than anything else to come to him. She felt absolutely ashamed that she had stumbled. She wanted more than ever to fix it. But she forced herself to ask again:

"No, I mean, are you from town? Are you a student at another ballet school? Why do you wear the same clothes every night? And why don't we ever go out?" She swallowed and asked the biggest, hardest, most important question. "Am I your girlfriend?"

Devon's expression softened, and he came to her again, pulling her close.

"Darling Giselle," he whispered in her ear, "there is no one else but you. You are my partner." He began to lead her in the same steps they'd danced before.

Ophelia relaxed into him and let the moves take her over. She didn't need to think. She didn't need to question him. She was the only one for him. He'd said it.

As the turned on the dance floor, Ophelia whispered, "I love you."

Chapter 11

The next day, Ophelia began to avoid her friends again. If they were going to be jealous and judgmental, so be it. She didn't need them. She had Devon.

All day, Kayley tried to catch up with Ophelia, but Ophelia always managed to get away.

Every time she saw Kayley, though, the questions her friend had brought up echoed in Ophelia's mind.

She moved through the day in a fog, feeling sharp and alert only once, when her stomach growled. She grabbed a snack out of the snack machine but forgot about it almost immediately. Thoughts of Devon and his kiss overwhelmed her every time she went to take a bite. The day crawled by so slowly that Ophelia wondered if she would ever make it to midnight. She barely registered it when Ms. Traysor, the history teacher, told her she was flunking the class.

She had never flunked a class in her life. But nothing else mattered now. Nothing but Devon.

Ophelia forced herself to go to the second ballet class of the day. Her body felt tired and weak, but thoughts about perfecting the part of Giselle propelled her to practice.

When she walked into class, Madame Puant was speaking to that same lady Ophelia had seen before, on the day she passed out. The woman looked hard at Ophelia once again, and Madame Puant glanced at her too, a disapproving look on her face. For a second, Ophelia was afraid Madame Puant had found out about her nighttime forays. But Madame just pounded her cane again and ballet class started.

At the end of class, Ophelia grabbed her bag during reverence so that she could skip out without having to talk to any of the girls. As she walked into the hall, she turned left instead of right and hid in an empty classroom while she waited for her friends to leave.

The classroom was dark, but a few sunbeams slid through the windows up high. The space had obviously been a science room—old beakers and test tubes lie everywhere, scattered and dusty. Ophelia shook her head. She'd been at the academy for three years, and still, she didn't know the school. Whatever else Kayley was wrong about, she was right that this place was special.

"I know what you've been doing at night."

Ophelia knocked into a side cabinet and glasses tinkled inside. The well-dressed lady Madame Puant had been talking to stood in front of her, one diamond-laden hand on a nearby table.

Ophelia tried to stop the hard beating of her heart. Yet again, the darkness started to fold in around her eyes at the edges.

"He makes you feel warm, but he's cold. Believe me. You feel like you're the only one, but you're not." Sadness crept into the lady's voice.

Ophelia regained her composure and said, "Who are you? And what are you talking about?"

The lady traced her finger on the table, lifting it up and looking at the pattern she'd made in the dust. She wiped her hands together and sighed.

"Ophelia. I am a friend. I'm someone who knows what you're going through. And believe me, if I could stop it, I would. But you have to end it yourself. That's just the way it is."

"I don't know what you're talking about," Ophelia said through clenched teeth. Though a part of her—a small, faraway part—knew exactly what the woman was talking about.

"My name is Jordan Johnson. I used to dance here."

Ophelia's jaw dropped open. Jordan Johnson. One of *the* Johnsons—the people who own Dario Quincy Academy. Back in the nineties, she had been the best dancer the school had ever seen. She was a legend among all the students in the place—the person Ophelia got compared to the most. Only, rumor said that Jordan had become ill during her senior year. She stopped dancing. No one knew why.

"Did you ever hear stories about why I left the school?"

Ophelia shook her head. "Only that you got ill."

Jordan nodded. "Yes, that's right. But my father made sure that no one knew why. You see, he didn't want to hear any more stories bandied about involving this school." Her face darkened. "Even if those rumors were true."

Ophelia wasn't sure what to say next, half afraid of what Jordan was about to tell her.

Jordan moved closer and clasped Ophelia's hands. "I left because I was ill. And I was ill because I was Giselle. My father decided to put on the ballet, despite the rumors of the curse. And I, of course, was thrilled to be the lead. I believed I could beat any curse that threatened me or the school."

Ophelia shifted on her feet as a wave of dizziness washed over her, but she waited it out and kept listening. "I thought the person who did Giselle died that year."

Jordan shook her head. "No. From what I can tell, the rumors have been a mix of truths and falsehoods for a while. My father couldn't conceal the fact that he had planned to put on *Giselle*. Too many people knew about that. However, he did what he could to protect my reputation—or his. To keep me from being part of the legend."

She went on, her head down. "I was close, though. To death, I mean. It was by sheer luck and love that I didn't die. Those before me weren't so fortunate.

"You see, very soon after rehearsals began, I met a boy. A beautiful boy who could dance like no other. And this boy and I would meet every night—every single night—to dance *Giselle*. Never before in my life had I felt such beauty. Never had I felt like I belonged to someone else. Never before had I been in love."

Ophelia's face burned. She dreaded whatever

would come out next.

"Have you been dancing with Devon, Ophelia?"

Ophelia backed up into the cabinet and heard glass break. "You have no idea what you're saying," she said. "You don't know him!"

She searched for her bag and for the exit. She had to get out of there.

Jordan spoke quickly. "He is not from this world, Ophelia. He will kill you if he can! He *is* killing you. Look at yourself! Stop dancing before it's too late!"

Ophelia found her bag and started to sprint. She heard Jordan yell behind her, "Read my diary! You'll see!"

But Ophelia was already out the door. She turned sharply and ran right into someone. Kayley looked up at her from the floor with worried eyes. Ophelia shook her head and ran down the nearest staircase, tears spilling over her cheeks. She made it to the kitchen of the house, hiding herself between the big industrial refrigerators. The cold made her feel good. Made her feel like she was with Devon.

Her crying turned into dry heaves.

She had to find Devon tonight. She had to make sure she was the only one, that what that woman had said wasn't true. She had to. She felt like her life depended on it.

Chapter 12

Once she was all cried out, Ophelia stood up slowly. She had to grab on to the handle of the refrigerator to stop from falling. It swung open, almost taking Ophelia with it. She was so weak she could barely hold on. The cold air rushed over her.

Ophelia saw food inside the fridge and thought briefly that she should eat something, but she wanted to get up to her room and hide. Her head was pounding.

She climbed the stairs with caution and finally made it to her room, collapsing on the bed. She could feel every rib sticking out. Her heart beat erratically.

***

After an hour or so, Ophelia took out her diary and began writing in it, detailing everything Jordan had told her. Tears streamed down her face again.

It just couldn't be. Devon was hers and hers alone. How did Jordan even know his name? Ophelia would ask him that night. He would have to answer her then.

She set her alarm for eleven thirty and slept.

When the alarm went off, Ophelia sat up groggily and checked the clock. Adrenaline coursed through her. It was time to meet Devon. Butterflies danced in her stomach as she thought about her questions. But it was time. She had to know if what Jordan said was true.

She put on her dance clothes, feeling like an old woman. In the mirror, her hair was lank and lifeless. Her eyes were dark and sunken in. Her cheekbones looked like they could cut glass.

Kayley was right: Ophelia did look like death.

She walked up to the studio and made it there by ten to midnight, but she just didn't have the energy to dance.

Ophelia stretched halfheartedly, and at twelve, she turned to the center of the room, determined to see Devon come in.

His voice came from a dark corner of the room: "My Giselle."

She turned slowly around to look at him. His pale eyes beckoned her, and before she could utter a word, he brought her toward him.

They began to dance.

After about five minutes, Ophelia knew something was wrong. She could barely stand up.

Stars danced before her eyes. Her breath came out short and panicky. She tried to get Devon to stop, but he kept whirling her around.

Finally, she broke away.

"Did you dance with Jordan Johnson too? With other girls?"

He smiled an indulgent smile and said, "I am always here for you. When you dance Giselle on the stage, I will be there for you too. We will be together, always."

Ophelia shook her head. She felt foggy and disconnected. "Jordan Johnson said you tried to kill her."

His once-sweet face contorted in anger. "How dare you question me!"

He grabbed her, then pushed her away. Ophelia had no strength left. She landed on the floor buttfirst, head snapping against the wood.

The lights in the studio snapped on.

Someone grabbed Ophelia's shoulders, and she tried to back up, scared that Devon was going to hurt her.

Kayley's face came into focus. "Ophelia! Ophelia, are you all right?"

Ophelia blinked rapidly, trying to get her bearings. "Devon?" she said, worried he'd left.

The faces of Madeleine, Sophie, and Emma came into view behind Kayley's.

"Devon?" Madeleine said. "Who's Devon?"

Kayley frowned and looked at Ophelia. "Devon is the one who tried to kill Jordan Johnson."

With that, Ophelia passed out.

Chapter 13

For the second time in two weeks, Ophelia woke up in the nurse's office. This time, though, she woke up to the faces of her friends.

"Nurse John," Kayley said, "she's awake."

Nurse John came into focus and said, "Ophelia, you passed out again."

Ophelia tried to croak, "Duh." But it just came out as a grunt.

The nurse patted her arm. "You just rest here. Your friends are going to look after you."

After he left, Ophelia found it hard to look at her friends. Silence overtook them, and no one moved.

Kayley was the first one to speak. "How do you feel?" she asked, putting her hand on Ophelia's arm. Tears came to Kayley's eyes.

Ophelia laughed a shaky laugh. "Like crap." She added, "What happened? . . . I don't know what's been happening."

Madeleine nodded and went to the other side of the bed, putting her hand on Ophelia's arm.

"You aren't getting enough nutrients, so they're giving you dextrose," Madeleine said. "Your electrolytes are off. Your heart rate's messed up too."

"That's the short version," Kayley said.

"You came close to, well . . . being really sick," Emma added.

Ophelia closed her eyes and let tears spill. She didn't open them when she murmured Devon's name.

When Ophelia did look up, Kayley stared down at her with compassion. "I overheard your conversation with Jordan Johnson. I heard about the diary. So we went and found it, in Madame Puant's office. It's super old-looking all right." Kayley held the diary toward Ophelia. "Don't even ask me how we snuck in there. Do you want to read it?"

Ophelia did and didn't. She couldn't bear the thought of Devon being with anyone else. She wouldn't believe that she was just another victim in a long line of victims. Or that Devon would hurt her in any way. But she remembered his look of anger and the way he shoved her. She swallowed hard and took the diary, opening it to the first page:

My friends are acting strange, and I know it is because they are jealous. The only thing that gives me comfort right now is Devon. Dancing with him makes the whole world disappear. I find that I long for him every single night—I wait with bated breath to be reunited with him. He feeds my soul like nothing else can. I needn't eat nor sleep, for Devon is my nourishment. Those around me only serve as distractions, and they will never understand this need I have for him, this yearning that consumes me.

Ophelia closed it with a hard *thunk*. The words were the same ones she had written in her own diary. Exactly the same. And she'd bet that the rest of the diary was at least as similar.

Her friends gathered around her and hugged her.

After a few minutes, Ophelia pushed them away and sniffled, reaching for a Kleenex. The rest of them reached for one too, and the five of them laughed together, a long, hard laugh. Ophelia realized it was the first time she'd laughed in ages.

It felt good.

When they finally stopped, she said, "You guys, I don't know what happened. I feel so . . . out of control."

She wiped her eyes impatiently. "It's just, no one makes me feel like he does. And I got so wrapped up in everything, I didn't even . . ." Ophelia sobbed again. "I'm so sorry. I've been so awful to all of you! I don't know how to let him go."

She told all of them the whole story. Every single bit. And for the first time in a long time, Ophelia felt light. She no longer had a secret, no longer had to sneak around. She was desperately afraid of losing Devon, but she knew that he wasn't good for her. She knew there was something up with him. And the only way to combat that was to get her friends involved.

If she had learned one thing at Dario Quincy Academy, it was that friendship trumped any curse.

When she was done telling the story, Kayley twisted her lips in thought. "We need to figure out a way to get him. But, Ophelia ... I don't think you should see him again. We'll all work together to find a way. Deal?"

Ophelia nodded her head slowly. "OK. But I will probably need to stay in someone else's room at night." She looked away guiltily.

Madeleine nodded. "Done. We have four nights until the performance, and you have four friends," she said. "It seems like we'll have just the right amount of time and people to figure this out."

"Thanks, you guys." She looked at each of the girls with complete sincerity. "You saved my life."

Chapter 14

"If we could just get Ms. Johnson's number, Madame." Madeleine blinked innocently.

Madame stared at her suspiciously. "Now what is this for? A class assignment on past ballet students?"

"Uh, yeah. For civics."

Kayley elbowed Madeleine in the ribs. Madeleine added quickly, "I mean history."

"Mm-hmm." Madame tapped her pencil on her desk. "And, Ophelia? You are well enough to complete homework assignments?"

Ophelia sank down in her chair. She'd skipped so many ballet practices, she thought for sure Madame would kick her out of the program. She'd even been hesitant to come to Madame's office. But she didn't want her friends doing anything that would get them in trouble—not without her, anyway.

She cleared her throat. "I'm feeling much better, Madame. In fact, I feel well enough to rehearse for the rest of the week before the performance. And speaking of *Giselle*, we saw you speaking to Ms. Johnson the other day while we were rehearsing. That's what made us think about her for this interview. It would be especially interesting because of her relationship to this academy." Ophelia looked directly in Madame's eyes. "And she might have a lot to say about the school and all the . . . interesting things that have happened here."

Madame's mouth turned up in a tiny smile before she became serious again.

"You know, that might be just the thing. If it's one thing I can't abide in this school, it's secrets. That and rumors. Unacceptable."

She stood next to Ophelia, putting her hand on her arm. "When we bring things out into the light, then we take away their power."

For some reason, tears came to Ophelia's eyes again. She felt like Madame saw and knew everything.

"Keep strong for the performance," Madame said. "But if there's a single hint that you are not well enough to do *Giselle*, the performance is canceled. You've already had one close call."

Madame sat down at the desk and scribbled something on a piece of paper. "Now, normally, I'm not in the habit of giving out the numbers of our board members. But for this, I'll make an exception."

She handed the number to Kayley and said, "As long as you girls work together, this will all be all right." She gave a slight wink that could have been easily overlooked. "Work together within the bounds of the assignment, of course. Now, carry on."

She looked down at her desk in a clear dismissal of the girls. As they walked out, she added, "Call from a school phone, please, not a cell phone. And I expect you'll be burning that number after you use it."

***

After two hours and lots of pacing, Ophelia finally found the courage to call Jordan. When she picked up the phone, Kayley threw her hands in the air. "It's about time!"

Ophelia bit her lip and dialed. On the third ring, Jordan picked up.

"Hello? This is Jordan."

Ophelia swallowed. "Jordan, this is Ophelia."

Silence greeted her at the other end. After a few seconds, Jordan spoke warmly. "Ophelia. I'm so glad you called. I know that took a lot of courage."

Ophelia nodded and then felt ridiculous because she was on the phone. She said, "Jordan, I read your diary and . . . I know about Devon. Or at least, I know what he's trying to do. He tried to kill you, didn't he?"

"Yes. He did. He had killed at least two others before me."

"How? *How* did he try to kill you?"

Kayley, Emma, Sophie, and Madeleine crowded around the phone. Ophelia elbowed them to get some air.

"He starts by making you feel special," Jordan began. "By making you feel you're the only one on the floor. The only one who can be his partner. But he sucks the life force out of you.

"I was the lucky one. My father saw what was happening to me in time. He pulled me out of the school and put me into therapy and a program. By that time, I could barely stand up. Those before me weren't so lucky."

"I'm so sorry," Ophelia said. She knew exactly how Jordan felt. "I dance Giselle this Saturday. What do I do to stop him?"

There was silence again on the other line. "You can't dance it. He'll kill you."

Frustrated, Ophelia said, "Well, how do I stop him?"

Jordan laughed. "You don't! You just don't dance it. You know Giselle's death scene? The dance that has all that footwork and all the leaps? That's when his victims died. You can't dance Giselle, Ophelia. It will kill you."

Ophelia thought about that for a moment. "Thank you for your time, Jordan. You really helped me."

"Ophelia, I'm truly sorry," Jordan said. "This isn't something anyone should have to go through."

Ophelia hung up. Madeleine patted her shoulder. "I'm so sorry you can't dance Giselle, honey."

Ophelia laughed. "Oh, I'm dancing Giselle."

The other girls said in unison, "What?!"

Ophelia laughed again, feeling giddy. "Yes, I'm dancing Giselle." She grabbed a granola bar, taking a huge bite out of it. "I'll be damned if I'm letting some stupid ghost boy stop me from living my dream."

Chapter 15

Ophelia felt strong. She felt the music flow all through her veins, felt it almost take her over. Almost.

She was herself now. And she was waiting for Devon to show up.

The performance was going to start in twenty minutes. She looked at Madeleine, Kayley, Emma, and Sophie, all of them nervous and shaky. Ophelia jumped up and down to get the blood flowing. She'd had a huge dinner earlier to make sure she had enough fuel for the performance. She peeked out from behind the curtain and saw Jordan Johnson and her father in the red velvet boxes that sat above the crowd. Ophelia could see they were nervous. Jordan kept wringing her hands, and John Johnson III bounced his knee.

A hand drew her back and she jumped.

It was Madame. Her face was pinched, and she beckoned Ophelia to follow her.

They went backstage, and the sounds of the orchestra warming up faded in the background.

Ophelia leaned against a cardboard house used for the second act and looked at Madame curiously. Madame took Ophelia's face in her hands. The move was so surprising, Ophelia had no words.

"Ophelia, you will tell me if this ballet is too much?" Madame said. "You will not go on if you think you'll get hurt, yes?"

Ophelia felt a lump in her throat. "I would tell you," she said. But a wave of doubt hit her.

"Ophelia. I know that whatever it is you fight tonight, you will win. I have full faith in you. And we are all here for you. Always."

Tears threatened Ophelia's eyes. She managed to say, "Thank you, Madame." Madame nodded and walked away.

Ophelia took a deep breath and said quietly, "I'm worried too, Madame."

She stepped back toward the staging area and the strains of the orchestra coming together. Someone yelled out the fifteen-minute mark, and Ophelia found Madeleine, Kayley, Emma, and Sophie.

The five girls grabbed each other's hands and formed a circle. Ophelia whispered, "Whatever happens tonight, you did everything you could."

Kayley huffed in anger. "You still don't have to dance this! Can I just say again, I think this is stupid? It's just a stupid ballet, Ophelia. It's not worth your life!"

Some other dancers looked over at them curiously.

Ophelia squeezed Kayley's hand. "I don't know how I know, but I do. If I don't face this now, it will haunt me forever. He will haunt me forever. Jordan isn't over him. I heard it in her voice. And I don't want to be like that. I think tonight is my night to break free. And I have to do it alone."

Sophie shook her head. "Not alone. We're here."

Ophelia smiled. "Yes. You're here. And after this ballet, I'll be here too." She squeezed their hands, and the stage manager called places.

Ophelia took her spot and prepared to dance for her life.

Chapter 16

After the first few scenes, Ophelia felt wonderful. She felt in control of the dance for the first time, felt the beauty of the movements and the heartbreak of the story. She felt everything she was supposed to. But Giselle's death was coming up, and she couldn't deny that she felt nervous.

And then she saw him. He was across the stage from her, staring at her with those beautiful pale eyes. She could almost smell him from where she stood: right by Madeleine, who didn't seem to see him. She noticed Madeleine looking her way and gave her the thumbs-up. Ophelia gave a halfhearted wave back.

Was she the only one who could see Devon?

The music that signaled Giselle's entrance to the death scene began to play. Across the stage, Kayley, Emma, and Sophie had joined Madeleine, none of them seeing the agent of death right next to them. They held each other's hands, staring at Ophelia with worried eyes.

When her time came to go onstage, Ophelia prepared for the battle of her life.

She entered on scene and sure enough, Devon came too, dancing with her for each step. She could smell his dusty scent, the woodsy, spicy smell that overtook her. Her eyes fluttered, she melted into him. She could feel like this forever.

He whispered to her: "Giselle. My Giselle."

She turned away. "I am not your Giselle."

When she pirouetted around, he was in front of her again. He grabbed on to her waist and held her close. It would be so easy to just give in. Just to let him have her so that she could feel this way forever; warm, comforted, perfect.

She glanced at the side of the stage and saw her friends standing there. They were still holding hands, worried expressions still on their faces. She knew that each one of them also held her right then, held her in their hearts. She knew they couldn't see Devon, and even if they could, they wouldn't be able to see what made him so irresistible. She loved them, she did. But maybe she loved Devon more.

He spoke softly in her ear: "It's time. Come to me, Giselle. Come to me forever."

Ophelia felt her heart flutter. Felt the beats slow as she danced. Felt her vision blacken. And she knew.

This was dying.

She was performing Giselle's last steps. She was Giselle. And she would die in this scene. She felt light and airy, felt like she could evaporate and it would be all right. It would be peaceful.

She saw a glimpse of Madame in the wings, saw tears running down her face. She thought about her friends and her family, about dance and her studies, about laughter and life. She thought about cold winter days and creepy hallways and springtime and lakes and sunlight.

And her eyes sprang open.

Tonight was not the night. It was not time. Tonight, Giselle would live.

She began to dance other steps. Steps that bounced. Steps and moves that put her firmly on the earth.

"What are you doing?!" Devon hissed at her. His face, once beautiful, looked grotesque.

All she could do was laugh. With each step, she felt her heartbeat grow stronger.

"Stop it! You're ruining it!" Devon screamed at her. He had started to fade.

The other dancers onstage looked confused. The corps had almost stopped dancing completely. For a moment, her resolve weakened.

But then she was surrounded by Madeleine, Kayley, Sophie, and Emma, and the five of them created a dance on the spot. A dance for life.

They danced Devon out of the circle. He howled in rage.

"You'll never be anything without me!" he yelled, circling around her like an animal. "You'll be nothing, I say, nothing!"

Ophelia did four fouettés in a row, and with each spot, she said, "I. Don't. Need. You."

By the last spot, he had disappeared completely.

She felt the hold on her loosen. Her heart beat strongly, and her vision cleared.

In front of her were four friends who stayed with her through everything. Who jumped onstage with her and made up a dance to kick out a demon.

This, she thought. This was something to live for.

And in the middle of the stage, in the middle of a ballet about a girl who dies, Ophelia hugged her friends and celebrated her life.

Epilogue

John Johnson III patted his head with a handkerchief.

"We were lucky, Madame Puant. Just lucky."

Madame Puant shook her head. "Not lucky. It was a show of strength."

Johnson stood up and leaned on her desk. "What if he comes back?"

Madame Puant sighed. "You and I both know he will. He always comes back. But for now, we can rest in the knowledge that one of our students beat him." She leaned forward. "And if she could beat him, then someone else can too. Now, don't you think that's encouraging?"

Johnson sank back in the chair. "Yes, I suppose you're right, Betsy." He chuckled. "You do seem to be right about almost everything here. I'll give you that."

"It's like I told you before, John. I know my students. And I would go to hell and back before I'd let something happen to them." She looked sadly out the window. "But we can't do everything for them. More often than not, they must help themselves. What we *can* do is be there for them, no matter what comes up."

She cleared her throat and then walked John Johnson III to the door.

"But I intend to do just that. I will be here. Always. No matter what."

THE DARIO QUINCY ACADEMY OF DANCE

Ballet. Gossip. Evil Spirits.

SEEK THE TRUTH
AND FIND THE CAUSE
WITH
THEPARANORMALISTS

About the Author

Megan Atwood is the author of more than fourteen books for children and young adults and is a college teacher who teaches all kinds of writing. She clearly has the best job in the world. She lives in Minneapolis, Minnesota, with two cats, a boy, and probably a couple of ghosts.